Carol Carrick

Patrick's Dinosaurs on the Internet

Illustrated by David Milgrim

Clarion Books · New York

Clarion Books, a Houghton Mifflin Company imprint
215 Park Avenue South, New York, NY 10003
Text copyright © 1999 by Carol Carrick
Illustrations copyright © 1999 by David Milgrim
Text set in 18-point Garamond BE Medium
Illustrations executed in Gouache
For information about permission to reproduce selections from
this book, write to Permissions, Houghton Mifflin Company,
215 Park Avenue South, New York, NY 10003.
Printed in USA
Library of Congress Cataloging-in-Publication Data
Carrick, Carol.
    Patrick's dinosaurs on the Internet /
by Carol Carrick ; illustrated by David Milgrim.
            p.   cm.
    Summary: After looking up information about
dinosaurs on his computer, Patrick is awakened by a
dinosaur who arrives in a spaceship to take Patrick to
his planet for show and tell.
    ISBN 0-395-50949-1
    [1. Dinosaurs—Fiction. 2. Interplanetary
voyages—Fiction. 3. Computers—Fiction.
4. Show-and-tell presentations—Fiction.
5. Schools—Fiction.] I. Milgrim, David, ill.
II. Title.
PZ7.C2344Patf   1999
[E]—dc21   97-47300
                        CIP   AC
WOZ 10 9 8 7 6 5 4 3 2 1

For Jack
—C. C.

To my nephew Jake
—D. M.

Patrick and his brother, Hank, were looking up DINOSAURS on the Internet.

"Ask where the dinosaurs are now," Patrick said, pulling on Hank's sleeve. He loved dinosaurs.

But Hank said, "I'm tired, and it's time to go to bed."

Patrick said, "Al-*read*-y?"

Hank turned off the lights, but Patrick lay awake watching the little stars on the screen saver. The stars arranged themselves into pictures—Ursa Major, the Great Bear; Pegasus, the Winged Horse; and Taurus, the Bull.

Patrick sighed. Too bad none of them were dinosaurs.

The stars blurred, and Patrick closed his eyes. "Dinosaurs, where are you now?" he asked softly. He imagined a herd of dinosaurs roaming across the Milky Way.

The computer beeped. The screen flickered, and Patrick opened his eyes. The freckled face of a dinosaur appeared. It looked right at him and answered in a friendly way, "WE'RE HERE WATCHING YOU."

"Hey!" said Patrick. "How did you get on my screen?"
"JUST KEEP YOUR EYES ON THE STARS," the dinosaur said.
"AND I'LL BE THERE SOON."

Then the screen went dark, and the little stars came out again. This time, one star was growing larger and brighter. Soon Patrick's whole room was bright, but now the light was coming from outdoors. He had to shade his eyes.

A spaceship hovered outside. Like a giant bumblebee it gently bumped his window. Its hatch door opened and a sign blinked on: WELCOME, PATRICK.

9

With a quick look, Patrick checked his brother—Hank was snoring gently. Patrick quietly raised his window, climbed up on the sill, and took one big step onto the spaceship.

The cabin was filled with switches, dials, and lights. "Have a seat," said the dinosaur at the controls. It was the same dinosaur who had appeared on Patrick's screen. "I'm Flato," he said. "It rhymes with Play-Doh."

"I'm Patrick," said Patrick. "It doesn't rhyme with anything."

Patrick fastened his safety belt. "Where are we going?" he asked.

"Where else?" said Flato, pointing to the stars.

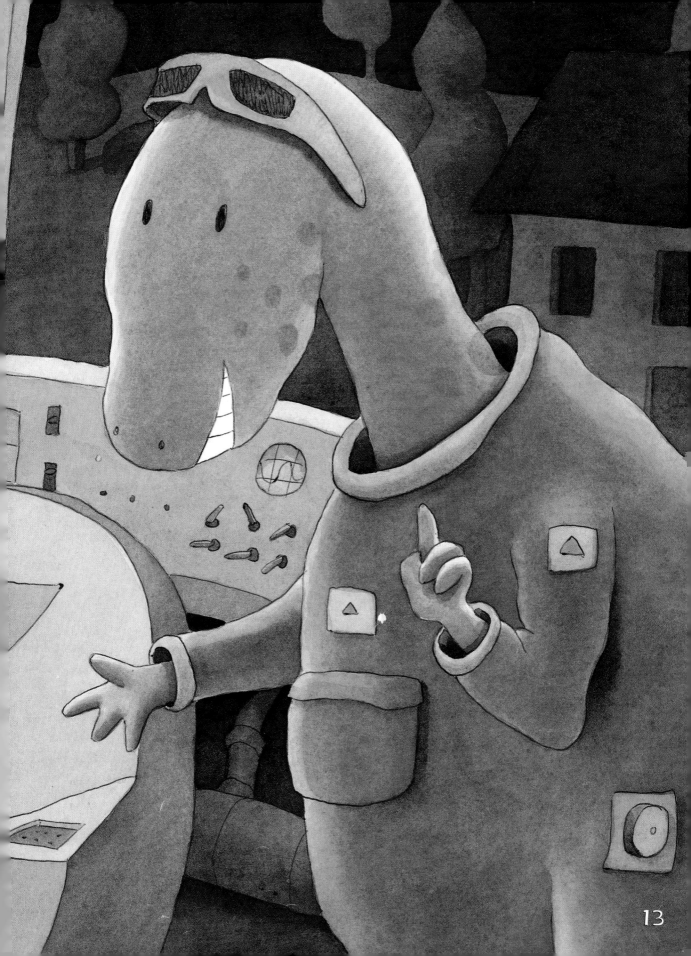

With a whirring sound, the hatch door closed. The roar of the engine grew deafening. Patrick was afraid it might wake up his parents and they would send him back to bed.

The spaceship trembled. It began to rise, higher and higher until the earth was a marble that spun beneath them.

"Would you like to drive?" Flato asked. "Go ahead."

Patrick took the controls. The spaceship swooped past cold, dark stars that snapped and popped like ice. It sped past the hot breath of glowing planets. "Neat!" he said. "Hank will never believe this."

"Here we are," said Flato, pointing to a small planet.

Flato took the controls as they flew over a school building. Below, Patrick could see classes of young dinosaurs and their teachers lined up on the playground.

The school band thumped a marching song as Patrick and Flato climbed out of the spaceship. The cheering squad shook their pompons, and the youngest class held up a banner that said: We Love You, PATRICK

Patrick stared in wonder. They were just like the dinosaurs in his books! "Brontosaurus," he said, "Stegosaurus. And my favorite, a Triceratops!"

Patrick was mystified. "How did they know I was coming?"

"We found you on the Internet," said Flato. "So I fetched you. You're my 'show and tell.'"

Flato's class was waiting inside. "Class, this is Patrick," their teacher said. "Patrick, will you show us on the map where you live?"

Patrick had to guess.

The dinosaurs wanted to know, "What is it like to be warm-blooded?" "Did you hatch from an egg?" "What is your favorite food?"

"Hot dogs," said Patrick, feeling hungry.

"Ugh!" said the dinosaurs. "He says he eats *dogs*."

"In our school we are plant eaters," the teacher said.

Then it was time for recess. The dinosaurs' favorite game was like soccer. "We play it the way you do," said Flato. "Only there's a penalty for standing on another player's tail."

Patrick managed to kick the big ball toward the goal. But the goalie, a very fat Triceratops, blocked it by sitting down.

There was a penalty for flattening the ball, but the goalie said he hadn't squashed it on purpose. The dinosaurs started to argue about that.

Suddenly there was a roar from the jungle. Then came the crack and crash of breaking trees. Heavy footfalls shook the ground under Patrick's feet.

The little dinosaurs scattered, but the teachers herded them back to their classrooms.

In the confusion, a shadow fell across Patrick. He knew this nightmare creature from his dreams—Tyrannosaurus rex. Patrick wanted to run away, but he couldn't. He shut his eyes and felt the dinosaur's terrible breath on his neck. "FLA-A-TO!" he yelled. "HELP ME!"

23

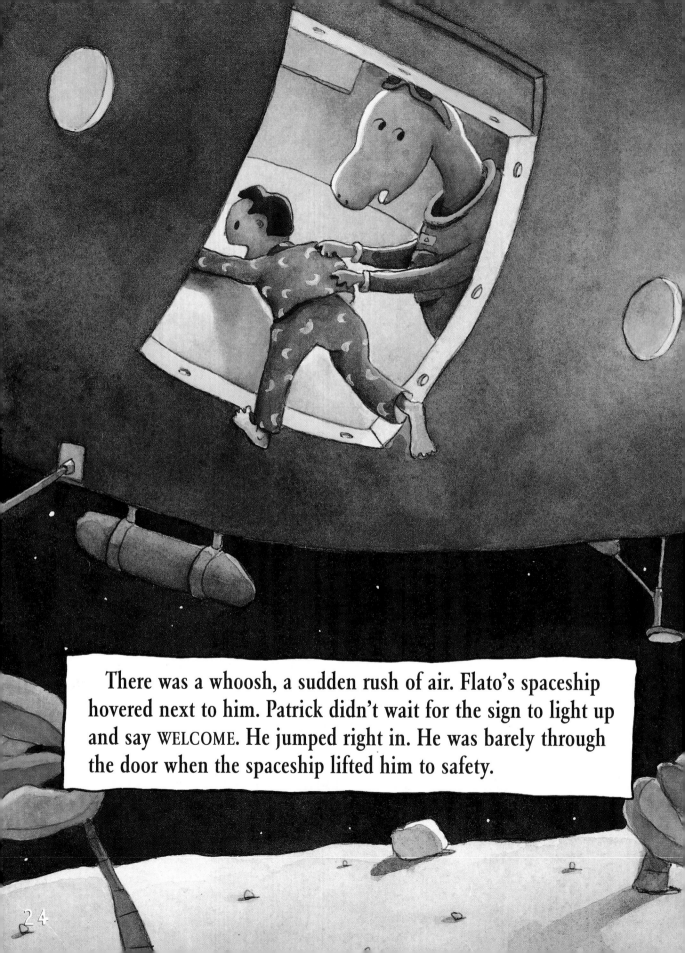

There was a whoosh, a sudden rush of air. Flato's spaceship hovered next to him. Patrick didn't wait for the sign to light up and say WELCOME. He jumped right in. He was barely through the door when the spaceship lifted him to safety.

"Look down," said Flato. Below them, the Tyrannosaurus rex disappeared into the jungle and the little dinosaurs ran out onto the field again. They waved to Patrick and shouted, "COME BACK SOON!" Patrick waved back to them.

"I was so scared!" he said.

"Aw, Rex probably wouldn't have hurt you," Flato answered. "He was just looking for handouts."

Patrick was puzzled. "What do you mean 'handouts'?"

"Until lately," said Flato, "Tyrannosauruses haven't been a problem. The few that are left stay in the jungle. But campers keep feeding them things like marshmallows and potato chips. So the Tyrannosauruses come out looking for more."

He turned to Patrick. "People tell me you have the same problem with bears in your national parks."

"People?" Patrick asked. "*Other* people have been up here?"

"Oh yes," said Flato. "We've brought a few to our planet, but they don't usually mention it back home."

I'd better not tell Hank, Patrick thought. *He'd never believe me.*

The world was coming into view. How cozy and familiar it looked.

"It's just as well that I'm taking you home now," said Flato. "You look sleepy."

Patrick *was* feeling sleepy. Maybe it was the hum of the spaceship or the bright starshine that made his eyelids heavy.

Soon they were skimming over his neighborhood. All the lights were still out in his house.

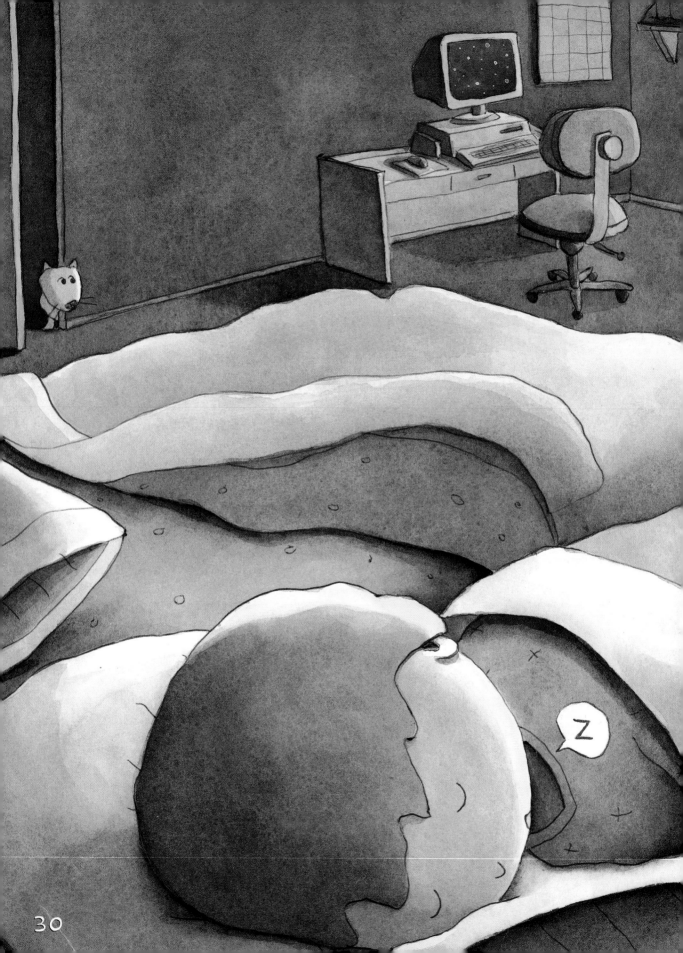

"I'll be in touch," said Flato as Patrick climbed through his window.

Patrick watched the spaceship leave. When it got too far away to see, he followed it on his computer.

The stars were blinking and arranging themselves on the screen—the Great Bear, the Winged Horse, and the Bull. But Patrick's eyes were already closed. Instead of stars, he was seeing dinosaurs.